P9-AOQ-912

Lost Souls

Also by Michael Collins

The Resurrectionists
The Keepers of Truth
The Man Who Dreamt of Lobsters (stories)
The Life and Times of a Teaboy
The Feminists Go Swimming (stories)
Emerald Underground

Dearest Ellie,

Why this small book? Because so often in the rough places you have reminded me of the "Good Tidings"; and made the way more smooth

A BOOK OF GOOD TIDINGS

And the angel said unto them,
Fear not: for, behold, I bring you
good tidings of great joy.

LUKE 2:10

A
BOOK OF
GOOD
TIDINGS

FROM THE BIBLE

JOAN WALSH ANGLUND

HARCOURT, BRACE & WORLD, INC.
NEW YORK

for my husband

bob

God is love.

I JOHN 4:8

But ask now the beasts, and they shall teach thee; and the fowls of the air, and they shall tell thee:

Or speak to the earth, and it shall teach thee: and the fishes of the sea shall declare unto thee.

JOB 12:7-8

To every thing there is a season, and a time to every purpose.

ECCLESIASTES 3:1

Whatsoever a man soweth, that shall he also reap.

By their fruits ye shall know them.

MATTHEW 7:20

And thou shalt love the Lord thy God with all thy heart, and with all thy soul, and with all thy mind, and with all thy strength: this is the first commandment.

And the second is like, namely this, Thou shalt love thy neighbor as thyself. There is none other commandment greater than these.

MARK 12:30-31

For God hath not given us the spirit of fear; but of power, and of love, and of a sound mind.

II TIMOTHY 1:7

I will lift up mine eyes unto the hills, from whence cometh my help.

My help cometh from the Lord, which made heaven and earth.

PSALM 121:1-2

Weeping may endure for a night, but joy cometh in the morning.

PSALM 30:5

This is the day which the Lord hath made; we will rejoice and be glad in it.

PSALM 118:24

God is our refuge and strength,
a very present help in trouble.

PSALM 46:1

Ask, and it shall be given you; seek, and ye shall find; knock, and it shall be opened unto you.

MATTHEW 7:7

When thou liest down, thou shalt not be afraid: yea, thou shalt lie down, and thy sleep shall be sweet.

PROVERBS 3:24

Have we not all one father?
hath not one God created us?

MALACHI 2:10